Mystery
Investigates

The Curse of the

Look out for more books about
Mariella Mystery

The Ghostly Guinea Pig
A Cupcake Conundrum
The Huge Hair scare

Mariella Mystery

Investigates

The curse of the
Pampered Poodle

by
Kate
Pankhurst

Orion
Children's Books

First published in Great Britain in 2014

Orion Children's Books
a division of the Orion Publishing Group Ltd
Orion House
5 Upper St Martin's Lane
London WC2H 9EA
An Hachette UK company

1 3 5 7 9 10 8 6 4 2

A catalogue record for this book is available from the British Library.

ISBN 978 1 4440 0894 4

Printed and bound in Great Britain
by Clays Ltd, St Ives plc

For Simon and Olive x

x-ray specs

me, totally ace detective

top secret

I ♥ MYSTERY

MYSTERY ALERT

THIS YOUNG SUPER SLEUTH JOURNAL BELONGS TO ...

MARIELLA MYSTERY: That's me! Need a mystery solving? As possibly the best detective around (who is aged nine and bit), get in touch with . . . you've guessed it . . . ME!

← me!

WARNING: This diary contains **top secret** and ultra-mysterious information for Mystery Girl eyes only.

← mystery Girl eyes only

MYSTERY NOTE: Can't find the toffee-flavoured yoghurt I was saving for my lunch. I suspect Arthur has eaten it. Could also have been Dad. One of them will crumble under questioning.

MISSING yoghurt (yum)

Monday
16th March

school trip today
YAY!

Puddleford museum

Lady Winkleton
on her adventures

**9:00AM
PUDDLEFORD PRIMARY, MISS CRUMBLE'S
CLASSROOM**

Today we get to see the famously cursed
Pampered Poodle of Puddleford. Curses are
totally mysterious, so the Mystery Girls are
investigating the poodle for our Museum
Mayhem project.

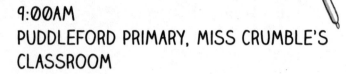

MUSEUM MAYHEM PROJECT NOTES

PUDDLEFORD MUSEUM: Celebrating being one
hundred years old. (Totally ancient.) They're
hosting the Museum Mayhem sleepover for
our school on Saturday night! (This afternoon,
our whole school is going on a research
trip to the museum to help us
prepare for Saturday.)

THE CHALLENGE:

To do a presentation about something from the museum's collection. The team that does the best one will win a totally brilliant prize — their work will be printed in the *Northern Star*, a really big famous newspaper. Poppy says if we win, this could really launch our detective careers.

THE TARGET: PAMPERED POODLE OF PUDDLEFORD (REAL NAME: MISTY)

Stuffed poodle that was once the much-loved pet of famous explorer Lady Penelope Amethyst Winkleton. After some creepy stuff happened with the poodle (more on that later), it was rumoured that anyone who heard Misty's bark would experience bad luck soon after.

misty ↑

(Really old photo of Misty)

woof

11

THE TEAM: THE MYSTERY GIRLS

NAME: POPPY HOLMES
ROLE: PRESENTATION PERFECTOR

Really good at performing in front of people (she's a champion synchronised swimmer). Says we've got the best chance of having the most exciting presentation because we've picked a cursed poodle to research.

poodle

poppy ↑

NAME: VIOLET MAPLE
ROLE: FACT OR FICTION OFFICER

Violet says that we will only win if our presentation is based on facts and we can't get carried away thinking curses actually exist because most are just made up. (I think she's a bit scared.)

violet (worrying)

12

NAME: MARIELLA MYSTERY
ROLE: FANTASTIC FACT-FINDER

I've had lots of practice
fact-finding during investigations.
It's totally going to help us win.

my best suspicious face

Poodles

annoying

**BEWARE OF MYSTERY
GIRL IMPERSONATOR:
ARTHUR MYSTERY (AKA
ANNOYING LITTLE
BROTHER)**

Arthur is researching the
Pampered Poodle's Dog's
Eye Diamond collar. I know he's only picked it
so he can follow us around pretending he is a
Mystery Girl. He never will be, though. Mostly
because he does embarrassing stuff. Like
making a rubbish cardboard diamond necklace
he's going to wear for the school trip.

Rubbish

13

The poodle is part of:

THE WINKLETON'S WONDERS EXHIBITION

THE PAMPERED POODLE AND DOG'S EYE DIAMOND

BUTTERFLY GIGANTOIDIUM FLUTTERUS

THE PICKLED SEA MONSTER OF PERU

DOG FORMATION DANCING

LADY WINKLETON DRESSING UP

BALLOON CURIOSITIES

GINGER GERTIE

WHAT WE KNOW:

WHO WAS LADY WINKLETON?

Penelope Winkleton lived in Puddleford one hundred years ago and was famous for going on crazy round-the-world expeditions. She founded Puddleford Museum and filled it with fascinating objects from her travels.

Lady W →

← misty

A MYSTERIOUS STRANGER:

Lady Winkleton often told the story of how she got her poodle from a mysterious stranger. The stranger said she could have the dog on one condition – that she MUST remain forever devoted to it or terrible things would follow. Lady W couldn't imagine not being devoted to such a gorgeous dog, so she agreed.

MISTY:

When Misty died of old age, Lady Winkleton had her pet stuffed, and kept her in her drawing room so she could remember her forever. To avoid being damaged, the newly-stuffed Misty was left at home when Lady W went on her next expedition.

That's when the **bad luck** started.

stuffed

misty

BAD LUCK AT WINKLETON MANOR:

MARYBELLE WIMPLE, LADY W'S MAID: After knocking Misty over while dusting, she heard a bark and one of the paintings fell off the walls.

Soon after, Marybelle was infested with a terrible case of fleas, fleas that could only have come from a dog. This was totally weird because there hadn't been any living dogs in the house for weeks, only a stuffed one! Marybelle was convinced Misty had cursed her.

GERALD SMYTHE, HEAD BUTLER: Bumped into Misty and heard a bark. Later that day, he tripped over a dog's bone and fell down a staircase. Nobody could explain how the bone came to be there. Misty's possessions had been tidied away weeks before.

bumped head

(For even more WEIRD bad luck stories from Winkleton Manor, see this shocking library book.)

THE lady THE CURSE AND THE POODLE

16

THE BAD LUCK GETS WORSE!

A few days into her last expedition, the terrible news arrived that Lady Winkleton had been eaten by a tiger. Definite **bad luck** alert!

Full →

MISTY TODAY

Lady W left all her possessions and fortune to the museum. The museum didn't want a cursed dog so the poodle has been on loan to other museums, until now. But the story of the curse has never gone away. Dad (top journalist at the *Puddleford Gazette*) says there have been loads of strange reports of **bad luck** in museums where the poodle has been displayed.

QUESTION: Could a stuffed poodle really be to blame for all these incidents of **bad luck**?

NOTE: I know it's probably just a made-up story but it will be TOTALLY amazing if there is a curse and the Mystery Girls manage to prove it after a hundred years!

17

RARE MYSTERIES: CURSES

Many people believe that stories of curses bringing bad luck and misfortune are superstitious nonsense. But for those involved, a curse can be troublesome, dangerous, and even deadly. Even though curses are rare, it's important to know how to recognise the signs of a curse mystery.

How Do Curses Work?

1. Somebody curses a person or an object. The type of people who usually make curses include:

you are CURSED!

A: Ancient Egyptians

CURSED!

B: Those desperate for bad things to happen to somebody else.

C: Those involved with witchcraft

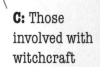

2. Some unusually bad and mysterious bad luck happens to the curse victim.

Detective's Dictionary: Curse Words

Superstition: This is when people believe there may be supernatural forces at work. Superstitious people are more likely to believe in curses and get hysterical without checking the facts first.

Coincidence: When bad luck happens, ask 'Was this just a coincidence? Or could it be curse related?'

Curse Protection

Rabbit's Foot

Four Leaf Clover

Bird poo: A bird pooing on your head is a lucky sign

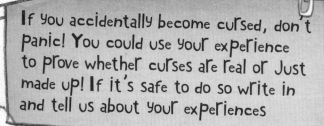

TOP TIP

If you accidentally become cursed, don't panic! You could use your experience to prove whether curses are real or just made up! If it's safe to do so write in and tell us about your experiences

Posh Poodle

10:10AM
PUDDLEFORD PRIMARY, MISS CRUMBLE'S CLASSROOM

The school bus won't be here for another hour, so we've been putting the finishing touches to our poodle surveillance plan – Operation Woof. Or at least, me and Violet have. Poppy has been trying to find out what the other groups are working on. She says we need to stay ahead of the competition.

"If we're going to investigate whether the poodle causes bad luck, we need to try and record it barking – so we've got proof," I said. "The poodle is supposed to bark when it's insulted or bumped into, so what about calling it a stinky poodle?"

"I'm positive that the curse stories aren't true," said Violet. (She didn't look positive.) "But what if we actually do get cursed by the poodle?"

Violet worries too much. The Young Super Sleuth's Handbook says calculated risks* are fine, and if we do get cursed, well, that could be really good for our research!

Just then, Poppy stormed back to our table. "I overheard Jane and Alice from Year Six in the girls' toilets," she said. "They're planning to sing a song about Lady Winkleton's collection of stuffed tortoises. Can you believe it? I think we might need to do a dance routine or we won't stand a chance."

dwarf tortoise

gurgle
gurgling tortoise

scaly tortoise

giant man eating tortoise

*CALCULATED RISKS: Thinking it through before doing risky stuff, like getting yourself cursed.

If Poppy spent more time reading The Young Super Sleuth's Handbook, she'd know it's important for detectives to look professional at all times. So there's no way I'll be dancing when we reveal that the Curse of the Pampered Poodle is real.

Poppy's inappropriate dancing

Anyway, the Mystery Kit is packed and I've even found this voice recorder in Miss Crumble's cupboard. It ribbits when you press record, but it should do the trick if the poodle does bark. You never know …

10:40AM
PUDDLEFORD PRIMARY, BREAKTIME

TERRIBLE NEWS!

The museum has just called Miss Crumble to cancel our trip. There is a problem with the alarm guarding the poodle and the Dog's Eye Diamond. The whole museum has been closed because it won't stop going off.

I wonder if the alarm problem might be something to do with the poodle's curse? Could somebody at the museum have annoyed the poodle? This certainly seems like a case of BAD LUCK.

annoyed?

23

"You are getting carried away, Mariella," said Violet, when I told her my theory. "The alarm is probably just broken."

"We could go and ask at the museum, to see if anyone heard anything weird before the alarm went crazy. Like a ... BARK!" Poppy said, making Violet jump out of her chair.

Poppy was winding Violet up, but actually it was a brilliant idea.

"That's exactly what we need to do, as soon as the museum re-opens. If anyone did hear a bark, they could be our first real-life curse victim!" I said.

So, actually, the museum visit being cancelled isn't so terrible. If the alarms going off are a sign the curse is active, that will totally help our investigation!

WOOOH! Museum trip back on!

Tuesday 17th March

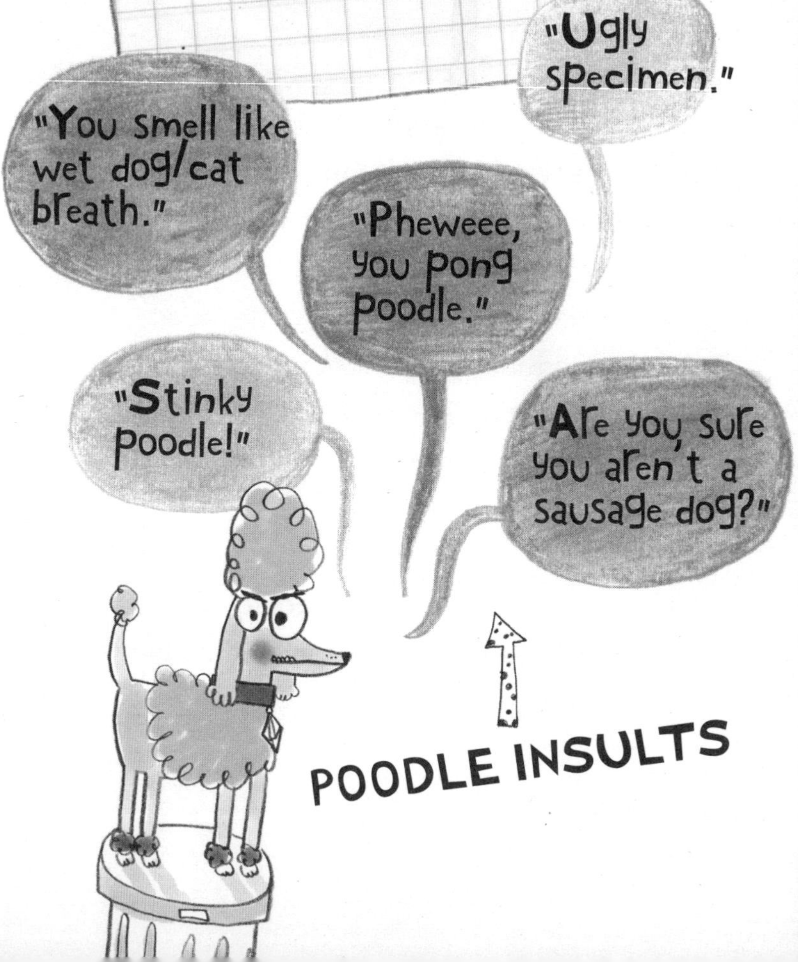

11:00AM
OUTSIDE PUDDLEFORD MUSEUM

I was so relieved this morning when Miss Crumble told us the museum alarms had been fixed and the trip was back on. The museum is getting ready to officially welcome our school, so we haven't been inside yet.

I don't mind though, because we've just watched the most AMAZING dog dancing display by Perfect Pooches Dog Agility Group.

The best by far is Jennifer in Year Three's dog, Rocky. Her mum can get him to do stuff like hopping on one paw and walking backwards. WOW! Jennifer says they've just bought the cool new collar Rocky is wearing to celebrate him winning the Disco Diva Dog Championships. If I had a sniffer dog I'd definitely teach it to do that.

DISCO DIVA DOG!

I asked the lady in charge of Perfect Pooches, Sasha, if she had any tips on dog training. (Could be useful if I ever get a sniffer dog.) Sasha showed me how she uses a special whistle to tell her dog Bert what dance moves to do. Humans can't hear them, but dogs' ears are loads more sensitive so they can. It's a bit like a secret message. Cool. (Bert is a poodle, but not a cursed one!)

Sasha

dog whistle

bum bag (dog treats)

Bert

11:25AM
OUTSIDE WINKLETON'S WONDERS GALLERY

I think Lady Winkleton would have loved the dancing dogs, but she would have been totally bored by Beryl the museum manager's welcome speech. The only interesting bit was when she mentioned the poodle.

"There have been calls over the years for the priceless Dog's Eye Diamond to be removed from what has been described by some as 'a fleabitten old dog', but we are proud to have preserved the wishes of Lady Winkleton, by keeping the diamond and the poodle together," said Beryl.

Beryl
(boring)

Beryl went on, "Besides, the collar suits Misty, and we wouldn't want to do anything to upset her. Not after all the stories – I'm sure you know what I'm talking about!"

Everyone laughed when she said that. They seem to think the curse is a big joke. Well, if we're going to prove the curse exists we need to find out if any weird stuff has been going on since the poodle arrived, especially after what happened with the alarms yesterday.

The Perfect Pooches trainer, Sasha, has just got up to speak and – totally amazing – she's Lady Winkleton's great-great-granddaughter!

Now I think about it, she does look a bit like Lady Winkleton. And maybe keeping poodles has become a family tradition?

same beauty spot

sasha

Lady W

"I never knew my great-great-grandma but I am so proud that she opened this incredible museum and that she pledged her vast fortune to keep it open for future generations," Sasha said.

Poppy looked at me. She nudged Violet. I knew what she was thinking. Sasha might not have actually known Lady Winkleton, but she's her great-great-granddaughter, so we should definitely speak to her about the curse.

12:20PM
WINKLETON'S WONDERS GALLERY,
NEXT TO THE PAMPERED POODLE

I was expecting the
Pampered Poodle
to be really creepy
in real life, but
actually she is a
bit cross-eyed and
has a funny expression
on her face. Poppy
said she looks as if she
is trying to do a poo.

cross-eyed

dusty

"Mariella, I don't like this,"
said Violet. "It's not too late
to pick something else to
research."

I can't understand
why Violet doesn't
get that a potential
curse is just too good
to ignore. I nodded at
Poppy, who held up
the Ribbit Recorder,
just like we'd planned.

Ribbit.

The recorder started to whir.

"EUURRGGGHH. I have never liked poodles!"
I said, quite loudly.

"Wait! The recorder is full!" said Poppy.

What? Poppy pressed the playback button.

Ribbit.

We listened closely, then suddenly we heard a
weird noise.

Ruff Ruff RUFF!

Violet sprang back, horrified. Poppy looked at me in confusion. We definitely hadn't heard a bark – so why was there one on the recorder?

"Ruff ... ruff ... ha ha, I am the cursed poodle of Puddleford and I am going to eat you on toast! AwooOoooooh!"

Hang on a minute. That's not a poodle. Poodles can't talk, and they don't sound like...

Arthur!

It turned out he'd filled the whole recorder with stupid messages. Which means he's been in Mystery Girls HQ again, where, as a non-Mystery Girl, he is definitely not allowed.

Arrrgghhh! He just doesn't understand that this investigation is serious! Well, he won't get away with this!

mystery
HQ

totally
banned

Ginger Gertie

12:35PM
WINKLETON'S WONDERS GALLERY, BY GINGER GERTIE (HUGE GINGER POLAR BEAR)

We waited a while, just to see if Misty was going to bark after that insult. Nothing.

"Maybe we should try one last thing. What about poking it?" Poppy said, reaching towards Misty.

"THE SIGN SAYS 'DO NOT TOUCH'," yelled an angry voice. A museum security guard was striding towards us. (Badge said his name was Stanley.) "You'll have those blasted alarms going off again and I don't need any more stress!"

Stress? Interesting.

DO NOT TOUCH the POODLE (or else)

"When you say stress, are you talking about the poodle's curse?" I said.

security Stanley

"There is no curse!" Stanley snapped. "What bothers me is having to guard that ugly dog's diamond and stop the alarm going off every ten minutes."

Violet gasped when Stanley called the poodle ugly. I glanced up. It looked back at me with its funny cross-eyed stare, but it still didn't bark.

"If I see any of you touching exhibits again, you'll be in BIG trouble!" Stanley said, storming off.

Arrrggggghh! The poodle has been insulted twice now – and nothing – so we still haven't got anything useful for our project. At least we know Lady Winkleton's actual great-great-granddaughter is in the museum. We are going to look for her now.

still no sign of the TOFFEE yoghurt!

1:10PM
PUDDLEFORD MUSEUM, LUNCH AREA

We couldn't find Sasha anywhere,
but just before lunch, we spotted
a museum attendant. (Badge said
her name was Daisy.)

Daisy Winkleton's Wonders Tour Guide

"Don't worry, kids, that old fur ball
isn't anything to be frightened of,"
she said, when we asked if she
had experienced anything weird.
"The curse is just a silly story."

Daisy →
(friendly)

"Has there been anything
unusual happening at the museum?
Any bad luck? What happened
with the alarms yesterday?"
I said. (Did we *look* as if we
were scared?)

coffee

Daisy laughed. "Oh, that.
As if anyone is going to
own up to spilling coffee
on the alarm control panel.
Beryl would go crazy with them!"

"So, you haven't heard any weird noises, like a
bark, for instance?" Poppy said.

"Not recently," said Daisy.

I asked if she knew where Sasha Winkleton was.
I explained we wanted to speak to her as part
of our enquiry and find out if she believed in the
old curse stories. "Sasha? I don't think she'll be
much help to your enquiry. She thinks the curse
story is as daft as I do. We were laughing about
it earlier."

Daisy continued, "I don't know where she is, but there's a cursed Egyptian mummy upstairs if you want to really spook yourselves!"

She did an impression of a mummy and a pretend spooky moan.

woooh!

cursed mummy

I can't believe nobody thinks the curse is real. Even Sasha. (I totally thought she'd know something useful.) And there's no sign of any cursed-poodle-related activity either. Just a very careless member of staff who likes coffee. Boring.

THE CURSE OF THE PAMPERED POODLE:
THERE DOESN'T SEEM TO BE ONE. (RUBBISH.)

Old-fashioned toilets

2:20PM
PUDDLEFORD MUSEUM, OUTSIDE GIRLS' TOILETS

Interesting development! As we were leaving the museum to go back to school, we overheard a potentially mysterious conversation. It was Daisy talking to Beryl, the museum manager, and Stanley, the security guard.

"There's no way I'm going back in the Winkleton room, not while THAT poodle is there!" said Daisy. She looked red-faced and upset, completely different from the jokey, smiley person we'd met earlier.

edgy

"I've just looked and everything is fine – you must have imagined it," Beryl said. "It was probably one of those school kids messing around."

Beryl

Stanley

"You shouldn't believe the stories, Daisy," said Stanley. "There are no such things as curses."

"This was real, it was. Look, I'm not locking up on my own tonight, OK?" Daisy said, and she stormed away through a door marked 'STAFF ONLY'.

URGENT NEW MYSTERY: WHAT HAPPENED TO SPOOK DAISY?

Poppy   Violet   me

SCHOOL BUS

2:45PM
SCHOOL BUS, TRAVELLING BACK TO SCHOOL

I didn't think we were going to get a chance to talk to Daisy. The buses had turned up and Miss Crumble was counting everyone on. Then, totally brilliantly, there was a Missing Pupil Alert!

While all the teachers were distracted, Poppy spotted Daisy on the steps outside the museum. When she told us what had happened, I understood why she didn't want to go back inside. Prepare for total poodle petrification*!

*Petrification: A word I have made up that sounds catchy when you say it with poodle. It means the same as petrifying — totally scary.

poodle
petrification

42

1:00PM: Beryl says Daisy can't have her lunch break until she tidies the Winkleton's Wonders Gallery. (Kids from our school have left it a mess.)

1:07PM: Daisy is alone in the gallery so while tidying the Dressing-Up Zone she decides to try on a wig styled in the same way as Lady Winkleton's hair.

Lady Winkleton wig

1:12PM: Daisy pretends to be Lady Winkleton and says in a posh voice, "Good gracious, poo-hoodle! You look like you need a flea bath, you disgusting old thing!"

Dressing UP Zone

wig

arctic explorer outfit

aviator explorer

deep sea explorer

skis

1:15PM: While hanging all the costumes back up, Daisy hears it. **RrrrRUF!** A bark, snappy and angry-sounding.

1:16PM: Daisy spins round and stares at the poodle. The poodle seems to stare back at her. Trying to shake off this horrible feeling, Daisy turns and carries on tidying. She can still sense the poodle's eyes on her. (C-R-E-E-P-Y!)

1:18PM: Daisy tells herself there was no bark and it must have been a floorboard creaking. The old stories are a load of rubbish, after all.

1:20PM: The gallery is silent — then Daisy hears something else. **GrrrRRRR!** A low growl! It definitely isn't a floorboard. The next noise she hears is a scream. Daisy realises that she is the one screaming.

1:21PM: Daisy races for the exit. She hears a crash behind her and turns. A huge portrait of Lady Winkleton and Misty has fallen from the wall. Even weirder, she is sure she glimpses the poodle MOVE.

VERDICT: Daisy insulted the poodle and experienced the same thing as Lady Winkleton's staff a hundred years ago — a mysterious bark in an otherwise empty room.

NOTE: Daisy has been warned there is a chance she is now CURSED and is about to suffer an incident of BAD LUCK.

<u>CASE OFFICIALLY REOPENED</u>

MYSTERY (STILL) TO SOLVE: IS THE POODLE ACTUALLY CURSED?

pencil from museum gift shop

5:00PM
MYSTERY GIRLS HQ, EMERGENCY MYSTERY GIRLS TEAM MEETING

We've been trying to figure out what to do next. Well, me and Poppy have. Violet was mostly staring into space, when suddenly she said, "The other night I saw a massive snake in my wash basket. It was really scary."

I wondered if it was code for something. She continued, "It was just a sock, but it really had me fooled. That must be what's happened here. Daisy got scared and imagined it all." Violet folded her arms, as if she'd solved the case.

A bark, a growl, a falling picture and a moving poodle? This definitely doesn't seem like the sort of thing anyone could have imagined. I have deduced that Violet doesn't want the curse to be true because she's scared.

She does have a point, though. The Young Super Sleuth's Handbook says to rule out the logical explanations before you jump to crazy conclusions (like a curse):

Logical Explanation One:

Daisy got spooked and imagined everything. But why did the picture fall off the wall when Daisy was nowhere near it? And Daisy didn't even believe the curse stories — would she be so easily scared?

moving poodle

Daisy

portrait

3 metres approx

3.5 metres approx.

(Possible) Logical Explanation Two:

Daisy heard a bark, but it wasn't the poodle. It was one of the dogs from Perfect Pooches outside, barking really, really loudly so you could hear it inside. (Violet thought of this, but it doesn't explain the falling picture.)

(Could BE true) Logical Explanation Three:

One of the other museum attendants thought it would be funny to scare Daisy. They pretended to bark and knocked the picture off the wall.

(Not so) Logical Explanation Four:
The poodle did bark. The curse is real and Daisy needs to watch out in case bad luck is coming her way. (Eeeeeek!)

VERDICT: Something suspicious is going on. We're going back to the museum after school tomorrow to investigate.

Wednesday 18th March

REVENGE COMPLETE: There was no way I was letting Arthur get away with the Ribbit Recorder stunt. Last night while he was showing Mum another rubbish Dog's Eye Diamond collar he'd made, I put the Ribbit Recorder under his bed. Now he totally thinks the barking he heard was the poodle, and that he is cursed – ha!

Ribbit

HA!

4:00PM
PUDDLEFORD MUSEUM, WINKLETON'S
WONDERS GALLERY

We need to find out if Daisy has experienced any bad luck but there hasn't been any sign of her today so far. Just a few kids from school looking at stuff for their projects in the exhibition.

Before we searched the museum, Violet said we should see if we could hear any noises from outside. (To test her theory that the bark was from one of the Perfect Pooches dogs.)

We were in the Lady Winkleton Dressing-
Up Zone, concentrating really hard, when,
suddenly . . .

WoohoooWOOhoowooHOOOh!

Violet screamed and Poppy
dropped the wig she was
holding. I spun round to see
who, or what, had set off
the poodle's alarm. Stanley
appeared behind us.

"You'd better not be touching that
dog again!" he shouted. "I don't know how I'm
expected to guard the diamond when I've got
that flipping alarm going off every five minutes."

He was being a bit unfair. We weren't even
standing next to the poodle. But – interesting.
The alarm has been going off. Was it just more
coffee being spilled, or could it be the work of
the cursed poodle?

"Actually, we've been investigating a strange report. I think you are aware of it – the Pampered Poodle barking?" I said loudly. (The alarm was still going off.)

"I'm fed up of people getting hysterical about that fleabitten mutt," Stanley shouted. "I've just had to throw the dog dancing team out. They were making a fuss about hearing a bark. They had dogs with them – what did they expect?"

Me, Poppy and Violet looked at one another. Another bark? Then I thought about it. Stanley was probably right. If the Perfect Pooches dogs had been in the gallery just now, it must have been one of them, not Misty.

Perfect Pooches

"Have the Perfect Pooches team been inside with their dogs before?" asked Violet. (Good question, Violet.)

"I wouldn't put it past that Winkleton woman. I've had to tell her to stop touching the exhibits three times now. She might be related to Lady flipping Winkleton, but that doesn't mean she can go round acting like she owns the place," Stanley said. (Even though the alarms had stopped, he was still shouting.)

Hmmm. It looks as if Violet's theory might be right. (Totally boring compared to a real-life curse, though.)

"Well, this museum won't look after itself," Stanley said. "If you've got any more questions, ask the tour guide, Daisy. When she gets back from her extended tea break, that is."

Where *is* Daisy?

tea break ?

dinosaur

Flying
dinosaur

4:5ØPM
PUDDLEFORD MUSEUM, PREHISTORIC
PUDDLEFORD GALLERY

BAD LUCK ALERT!

We searched the museum for ages with no sign
of Daisy.

"She's probably gone home," said Violet.

But I know from Dad that you can't just go
home if you have a job, so Daisy must
be somewhere in the museum.
And I was right.

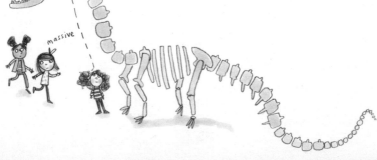

massive

As we walked past a giant dinosaur skeleton in Prehistoric Puddleford, I heard a faint voice.

"HELP! Somebody help meee, pleeeease!"

"Did you hear that?" said Poppy.

It sounded as if it was coming from a door marked 'STAFF ONLY'. And it sounded quite a lot like Daisy.

"Come on, girls – Mystery Girl assistance needed!" I said, pushing open the door.

"I don't like this!" said Violet. "We can't go in there, we'll get into trouble!"

The Young Super Sleuth's Handbook says detectives shouldn't worry about getting into trouble, because sometimes you have to if you want to solve a mystery.

Me and Poppy ignored Violet and stepped into a long, dimly-lit corridor filled with boxes. At the end was another door, and I could just make out the word 'STAFFROOM'.

It was totally spooky. I heard Violet breathing shakily behind me.

"Daisy? Is that you? Don't worry – the Mystery Girls are here," I called, as we reached the door.

The staffroom was dark and dusty. There were cobwebs hanging from the ceiling and broken furniture. We couldn't see Daisy anywhere. As we edged into the room, a huge hairy spider scuttled across the floor.

Huge

"Yeeeeekkkkk!" Violet's shriek echoed through the silence.

"Hello? Is someone there? I'm TRAPPED!" said the voice. It seemed to be coming from the Ladies' Toilets in the corner.

I ran forwards and swung open the door – into pitch blackness. What was Daisy doing in a deserted, dark toilet? I half-expected the furry paw of the pampered poodle to grab me as I tried to find the light switch.

CLICK.

The lights flickered, like something out of a scary film, then came on. Violet screamed again (highly unprofessional), and Poppy elbowed her.

"Mariella, Violet, Poppy? Is that you?" Daisy yelled. "I didn't think anyone was going to come. It's the curse, THE CURSE HAS STRUCK!"

calming cup of
museum
tea

5:15PM
PUDDLEFORD MUSEUM CAFÉ

The Young Super Sleuth's Handbook says
creating a relaxing environment really helps to
calm people down, so we've brought Daisy to
the museum café. She has told us everything.
Extreme creepiness overload!

CASE REPORT:
BAD LUCK INCIDENT: DAISY MEADOWFIELD

2:45PM: Daisy is worried about the curse
and has avoided going anywhere on her

own all day. But now she is
desperate for the loo, so she
decides to risk going to the
disused toilets in Prehistoric
Puddleford.

2:50PM: Daisy dashes into the cubicle. Is that a shuffle she can hear outside the door? Daisy tells herself she's just a bit jumpy.

2:52PM: The lights flicker, then go out. The toilets are plunged into darkness. Daisy can't even see the toilet roll. Her heart starts to race.

FEAR

2:53PM: Daisy tries to open the door. It's jammed. Then she hears it – **RrrrRUF!** The same angry-sounding bark she heard yesterday. She screams and falls back onto the toilet seat.

2:55PM: Daisy rattles the door and cries for help. Nobody comes.

4:45PM: The Mystery Girls arrive – Daisy has never been so relieved.

<u>**VERDICT:**</u> Daisy has suffered a definite incident of bad luck. Has she been cursed?

EMERGENCY MYSTERY GIRL SEARCH OF THE SCENE NEEDED!

CONDUCTING A SEARCH

An expert search of a crime or mystery scene can reveal evidence to solve the case. It's important not to get carried away with the thrill of the search and anticipation of solving the case though – this could lead to less experienced detectives missing vital clues.

Search: Dos and Don'ts

Finger Print Kit

X-ray Specs

DO use appropriate equipment to reveal clues.

Magnifying Goggles

DON'T accidentally contaminate the scene with anything. (Including, crumbs, pet hair and lost buttons.)

Hair Net

DO keep a record of everything you find.

DON'T Leave sniffer dogs unattended (Can lead to destruction of important evidence.)

Important Evidence

Searching the Scene: What to look out for

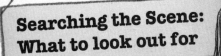

Who put that there?

(GUILTY)

Footprints: Can be used to reveal the dress sense of your suspect.

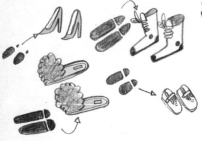

Planted Evidence: Has somebody deliberately left evidence to throw you off the scent?

False Teeth: Would suggest your suspect is a granny or a person who eats too many sweets

Concealed Criminals: Watch out, you could have disturbed the criminal at work. Are they about to ambush you?

SWAG

TOP TIP

Why not use some Young Super Sleuth crime scene tape to cordon off the area you are searching to avoid passers by trampling or contaminating evidence?

KEEP OUT MYSTERY IN PROGRESS

eeeek!

5:45PM
DISUSED STAFFROOM LADIES' TOILET, PREHISTORIC PUDDLEFORD

The museum is about to close but there was no way we were going to miss an opportunity to look for evidence. Here's what we found:

EVIDENCE FROM THE BAD LUCK SCENE

MYSTERIOUS PAW PRINT:
Is this the paw print of the pampered poodle? The only other dogs around the museum were the Perfect Pooches Dog Agility Group — and what would they have been doing in a deserted toilet?

cursed poodle's footprint ?

location of footprint

LIGHT SWITCH: Working normally. Light bulb works too. Could it have gone off on its own?

lightswitch

TOILET LOCK: Had mysteriously fallen off. Was it already broken or was this the work of the poodle?

fallen off

VERDICT: If we can prove we've found the paw print of the Pampered Poodle, we'll have something that connects Misty to the scene of Daisy's bad luck. Something to prove the curse stories are true.

PET EXPERT NEEDED: To help us analyse our evidence we are going to Mrs Finn (owner of Fluff 'n' Feathers pet shop and Mystery Girl supporter). The pet shop will be shut now so we'll have to go after school tomorrow. Arrrgghhh! Detectives shouldn't have to go to school!

Fluff 'n' Feathers

NOTE: Mrs Finn has a pet poodle. I bet she'd know a poodle paw print anywhere.

spangle

6:15PM

PUDDLEFORD HIGH STREET, OUTSIDE THE PICKLED PEPPER CAFÉ

I actually can't believe what just happened. Things aren't just weird now, they are full-on TOTALLY SUSPICIOUSLY MYSTERIOUS.

Walking home through town, we bumped into the dog owners from the Perfect Pooches Dog Agility Group. Great! I thought. We could finally speak to Sasha.

64

But quickly my Mystery Senses tuned in.
Something wasn't right.

"HAVE YOU SEEN ROCKY?" screamed Sasha.
Bert was pulling at his lead,
yapping wildly.

"He's gone!
VANISHED!" cried
Jennifer's mum.

What did they
mean?

I tried to sound calm
and confident, which was
hard over all the yapping.
"We are trained detectives," I said. "Tell us
exactly what happened."

EYEWITNESS REPORT: MYSTERIOUS DOG DISAPPEARANCE

WITNESS: Sasha Winkleton

MISSING!

DOG IDENTIFIED AS MISSING:
Rocky. Crossbreed, black floppy hair. Wearing new purple-studded collar. Owner — Joyce Johnson (Jennifer from Year Three's mum).

ROCKY

3:30PM: The Perfect Pooches Dog Agility Group finish their dance display and decide to look at the Winkleton's Wonders exhibition. They don't think anyone will mind their well-trained dogs being inside.

3:35PM: Spotting the Pampered Poodle. Joyce says Misty should have been called the Dishevelled Doggy instead of the Pampered Poodle. Everyone laughs. Sasha says the poodle stares at them in a really weird way.

3:40PM: They are looking at Lady Winkleton's collection of poisonous toads when they hear it. **RrrrRUF!**

Weird stare

3:41PM: Each owner is convinced it wasn't their dog. Joyce jokes that it must have been the poodle. Sasha has a funny feeling. (She's never liked Misty but doesn't often admit that in case she looks silly. She said that's why she was joking about it with Daisy.)

3:45PM: Stanley tells them that dogs that are not stuffed are strictly forbidden in the museum. They decide it's time to leave.

Funny feeling

4:05PM: Walking along the High Street, Sasha feels uneasy but tells herself she is being silly.

4:10PM: Rocky suddenly lets out a crazy-sounding howl. Sasha grabs treats from her bum bag to distract him.

treats

awoooh!

4:11PM: Without warning, Rocky lurches forward, pulling his lead free from Joyce's hand. Joyce shouts, "NO, Rocky, come here!" Rocky ignores her and runs off. Sasha can't believe it – Rocky always comes back when he's called.

4:16PM: Rocky has VANISHED. Joyce Johnson says she must be cursed for insulting the poodle earlier and this is the bad luck.

VERDICT: We can't be totally certain that Rocky's disappearance is connected to the curse. What we can say that it is TOTALLY MYSTERIOUS that, twice now, people have heard a bark from what they think is the Pampered Poodle, then suffered BAD LUCK.

curse victims?

Daisy   Joyce

6:30PM

PUDDLEFORD HIGH STREET, OUTSIDE STUFFED (CAKE SHOP)

We already have the paw print linking the poodle to the scene of Daisy's bad luck (we think), so Violet said it was imperative* to look for poodle-related clues at the scene of Rocky's disappearance too.

"Look at this!" Poppy said. She was pointing to a pile of dog poo. "If the poodle leaves paw prints it might leave poo too."

*Imperative: Totally vitally important and needs doing NOW!

POO!

"Euurrrgghhh! That isn't a clue – any dog could have left it there," Violet said.

"Have you found Rocky?" Sasha Winkleton said, running over. Her face wrinkled when she saw the poo. She obviously thought we were silly kids messing around.

"Sasha," I said. "You'll think this is crazy but we believe this poo could be evidence. We're looking for clues to link the Pampered Poodle to this location, to find out if Rocky's disappearance is curse-related."

yuck!

Sasha looked puzzled for a minute, then she smiled.

"Ooh, well done, girls," she said. "I like a good mystery story myself. I'm sure that poo could be relevant – it looks fresh, but it can't be any of the dogs from Perfect Pooches. We always poop-a-scoop. And I haven't seen any other dogs in the area since Rocky disappeared. "

Poppy looked really pleased. It didn't seem like a brilliant piece of evidence, but before Sasha poop-a-scooped it (we obviously can't keep poo), I took a photo to show Mrs Finn. Maybe she can confirm if it's from a poodle or not.

poo-tentially important evidence

As we were leaving, Sasha said something else interesting. "It's about time somebody investigated that poodle properly. There's lots of stuff people don't know about. Being the only living Winkleton, you get to hear about these things, but I wouldn't want to scare you all."

"Don't worry, we can take it," I said.

"To solve this case, you need to know everything. That poodle is capable of terrible, terrible things," Sasha said.

"Like what?" Poppy asked, nudging me. This was getting exciting.

"Well, at the last museum the poodle was exhibited, a museum attendant went missing. She was found days later, absolutely terrified and locked in a disused storeroom. This was after she'd bumped into the poodle, and heard a mysterious bark," said Sasha.

Me, Poppy and Violet all stared at each other. It was almost exactly what had happened to Daisy. No way!

shocked!

Sasha continued, "It gets worse. Let's just say a security guard, who was overheard calling the poodle 'mangy', doesn't work there any more. Not after an escaped lion from a local zoo got inside the museum."

Violet gasped. "He was eaten? Like Lady Winkleton?"

"Exactly," said Sasha. "There's no proof the poodle caused any of it, of course. Only rumours. But there's no smoke without fire, as my dad used to say."

"Woah," said Poppy.

Sasha has said she'll help the investigation in any way she can. She also said she'd love to find out more about real-life detectives, like us. Wow! She thinks we are proper detectives!

the mystery Girls

PROPER DETECTIVES

Thursday
19th March

NOTE: We should warn Stanley at the museum to stop insulting the poodle, especially now we know what happened to that other security guard.

stuffed poodle

8:15AM
PUDDLEFORD PRIMARY, PLAYGROUND

I've been trying to make sure we are totally prepared for our visit to Fluff 'n' Feathers.

"We need to ask Mrs Finn whether the paw print and the poo are definitely from a poodle. Are there any other questions we should ask?" I said.

I glanced at Poppy, who hadn't said anything for a while. This was strange, as she usually loves creepy stuff. Then I noticed she was staring at Jane and Alice from Year Six.

Jane was holding up a big green blob collage. I think it was meant to be a stuffed tortoise from the Winkleton's Wonders Gallery.

Jealous

man-eating tortoise

↑ Rubbish!

"Poppy! Are you listening?" I said.

"Oh, sorry, Mariella. I knew you would be busy thinking about the case, so I did a bit of work on our presentation for the Museum Mayhem project last night. Look at this!"

Poppy reached into her school bag. What she pulled out took my breath away. Violet screamed.

In front of us was a life-sized replica of the Pampered Poodle, complete with weird creepy eyes. Poppy made it from papier mâché. It's painted black, with hair stuck on in clumps. Eurrgh!

Fake Misty

toilet rolls?

"Brilliant! That's just the sort of reaction I was after!" said Poppy. "I thought this could really give our presentation the edge."

This isn't going to help the investigation at all, but I'm impressed by how realistic it looks. (And even though the case is more important, it would be amazing to win the Museum Mayhem project.)

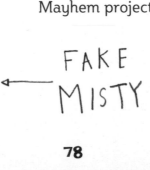

FAKE ← MISTY

3:45PM
BACK ROOM, FLUFF 'N' FEATHERS PET SHOP

We hoped our visit to the pet shop would give us some more clues, but we never expected this.

I knew Mrs Finn had made a really cool Winkleton's Wonders window display because Mum knitted a poodle to go in it. (Mum owns an online knitting shop – Knitted Fancies.) It had looked amazing. But when we got there, the knitted poodle was lying on its side and the Winkleton's Wonders sign was wonky too. Then I spotted the closed sign on the door.

Pet shop window

What was going on?

"Hang on," said Violet, peering through the window. "I can see Mrs Finn."

Poppy and me peeped over Violet's shoulder. It looked as if there had been a huge pet party or something – there were dog toys everywhere, bags of spilled food, dog beds upside down.

Mrs Finn jumped when she saw us.

"Oh, girls, it's you. You startled me. I'm a bit on edge – there's been a break-in," said Mrs Finn. "I'm not having much luck at the moment, with this, and that unfortunate incident at the museum yesterday."

An incident at the museum? A break-in?

"Mrs Finn, you don't need to worry. Tell us everything, starting with your visit to the museum," I said.

CASE REPORT: FLUFF 'N' FEATHERS SUSPECTED CURSE-RELATED BREAK-IN

WEDNESDAY

1:00PM: Mrs Finn arrives at Puddleford Museum. She's nipped out on her lunch break to see the Winkleton's Wonders Gallery.

mrs FINN

Winkleton's Wonders

1:10PM: It takes Mrs Finn a little while to find the exhibition because she's forgotten her glasses and can't see where she is going.

mrs finns glasses

1:15PM: Mrs Finn is heading for what she thinks is the ginger polar bear her customers have told her about, but doesn't see one of the displays right next to her. She bumps into it. An alarm goes off, really loudly.

knocked over

1:17PM: A security guard comes over and starts shouting at Mrs Finn. Mrs Finn can't believe what she's done. She is so embarrassed. She apologises and heads straight for the exit.

get out

1:22PM: On her way out, Mrs Finn hears a funny noise over the sound of the alarm. **Rrruufff!** Mrs Finn knows about the curse but doesn't believe it could possibly be true. She thinks it must be her imagination playing tricks on her because she is stressed.

stressed

THURSDAY

8:00AM: Mrs Finn arrives at work to discover there has been a break-in. The dog section has been raided. The window display has been messed up too. And something else has gone. The most expensive item in the pet shop – the diamante collar worn by the knitted poodle in the display.

diamante collar

3:10PM: Detective Sparks from Puddleford police finally arrives. He says there is no sign of a forced entry and he suspects Mrs Finn has forgotten she sold the dog treats and collar. She probably accidentally knocked a few things over when she didn't have her glasses on.

VERDICT: Mrs Finn is the THIRD person we know who has offended the poodle (even though she didn't mean to) and experienced bad luck. We strongly suspect she is another victim of the poodle's curse.

CURSE VICTIM?

Fluff'n'feath

mrs finn

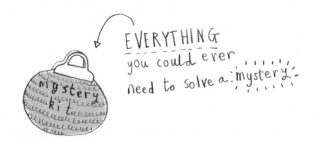

EVERYTHING you could ever need to solve a mystery

mystery kit

4:45PM
DOG SUPPLIES AREA, FLUFF 'N' FEATHERS
PET SHOP

NEW EVIDENCE ALERT!

Mrs Finn said we could search the shop before she tidied up properly. We looked all over and didn't find anything useful. Suddenly, Violet shouted, "Mystery Kit! I need the Mystery Kit!"

She'd spotted something on the wooden board behind the window display. Good work, Violet!

hair

"I think it's dog fur," Violet said, picking up a clump of curly black hair with a pair of tweezers.

"Goodness!" said Mrs Finn. "Well, that does look like poodle hair. And it can't be from my poodle, Spangle – he's grey."

We gathered around to get a closer look.

Then, out of nowhere, Poppy shouted, "POODLE ALERT!" What was she going on about? Couldn't she see Mrs Finn was in a state of shock?

"WHERE?" Mrs Finn gasped, looking around the shop.

Poodle alert!

"No, sorry,
I meant
here – it's a
paw print!"
said Poppy,
pointing at the
floor next to Violet's

feet. There, in some spilled flea powder, was a
paw print. It was so faint we'd almost missed it.

"I don't understand how that got there. The flea
powder was knocked over last night, and Spangle
hasn't been in the shop today. No dogs have,"
said Mrs Finn.

The shop locked from the inside. A stolen fancy
collar. Fur. Another paw print. Was this the
concrete evidence we'd been looking for?

"Mrs Finn. We need your help analysing this –
and some other stuff," I said.

"I'm going to need my glasses," said Mrs Finn.

FACT FILE: POODLE EVIDENCE

EXHIBIT A: POODLE PAW PRINTS. Located at bad-luck scenes of the Ladies' Toilets in Puddleford Museum AND in Fluff 'n' Feathers pet shop. Mrs Finn confirmed these could be from the same dog, and that they are the right size for a medium poodle, like Misty.

VERDICT: Not concrete evidence. People could say they were made by a normal dog, not a cursed one.

approx 7cm

FLEA

pet shop PAWprint

toilet PAWprint

approx 7cm

popular poodle hairstyles

EXHIBIT B: THE POO-TENTIAL POODLE POO.

Located at the scene of Rocky's disappearance.

Mrs Finn says a dog's poo size
depends on how big a meal they
have eaten. This is quite a small
pile. She says the Pampered Poodle
may not have eaten much, being
stuffed and living in a museum,
so it could be Misty's.

VERDICT: Not concrete evidence. Could have
come from any dog.

EXHIBIT C: SUSPECTED POODLE
FUR. Located in Fluff 'n' Feathers.

Poodle
fur?

Poodles have very distinct, dense
curly fur. Mrs Finn is confident this is poodle
fur. (She'd know it anywhere because her dog,
Spangle, is a poodle.) Did the poodle get its
fur caught while stealing the collar?

VERDICT: Could potentially be from another
black poodle, but Mrs Finn said she can't
remember the last time one was in her shop.

5:45PM
MYSTERY GIRLS HQ

The poodle is out of control!

We were back at HQ trying to figure out what to do next when Sasha came running down the garden. She looked flustered. I thought maybe she'd heard something about Rocky.

(We usually only get Arthur hanging around, not actual proper witnesses coming over. Yay!)

"I didn't know who else to come to – Beryl won't listen!" Sasha called up to us.

Her hands were shaking as she passed me today's edition of the *Puddleford Gazette*.

MAYHEM AT THE MUSEUM

It's been the most hotly anticipated exhibition at Puddleford Museum for years, but after today's shocking incident, many are calling for the Winkleton's Wonders exhibition to be closed due to concerns about safety – and about a certain cursed poodle.

The fallen polar bear – Ginger Gertie

This afternoon it was reported that a seven-foot stuffed ginger polar bear, known as Ginger Gertie, toppled over, almost crushing museum security guard, Stanley Mumble.

Stanley escaped unharmed, but refused to comment when asked about safety concerns at the museum.

Stanley Mumble

His colleague, Daisy Meadowfield, spoke out: "Stanley refuses to admit it, but I know this is the Pampered Poodle's work. I heard Misty bark. I got trapped in a toilet because of it. It was terrifying."

Daisy Meadowfield: Museum Tour Guide

We confronted museum manager Beryl Bottomly about whether the exhibition and a planned sleepover for local school children should go ahead amid rumours of a curse.

"I'm sure your readers are intelligent enough to know that this curse story can't possibly be true. What happened was an unfortunate accident."

Was this an unfortunate accident or are claims that the Pampered Poodle's curse is at work really true?

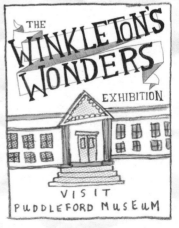

I knew we should have warned Stanley about insulting a poodle! It was only a matter of time. I wish Daisy hadn't mentioned getting stuck in the toilet. Written down like that, it just sounds silly. It's going to be even harder to persuade people the poodle is dangerous now.

dangerous!

tomato sauce

fish fingers and chips

6:30PM
MY HOUSE, 22 SYCAMORE AVENUE, KITCHEN

I can't believe Mum has made us come inside for dinner. I can't think about fish fingers and chips at a time like this! At least we didn't have to sit with Arthur. Mum said if we were going to carry on our meeting about the cursed poodle, she didn't want us putting any more silly ideas in his head before the museum sleepover. He's eating his tea in the living room.

Thanks to Mrs Finn and Sasha, we're pretty sure the poodle is totally cursed. The trouble is, now we need to prove it and stop anything else unlucky from happening. But how?

"I don't like this," Violet said. "If the poodle really is cursed, it could come for us next."

"That would be a fantastic way to get the evidence to win us the competition!" said Poppy. "Actually, I've had an idea about how we can use Fake Misty to really shock everyone at the sleepover."

We haven't even got a proper plan but Poppy has been going on about making a toilet cubicle from cardboard for at least ten minutes now.

Poppy's idea

Fake Misty

Violet

Poppy

Mariella

FEAR!

6:47PM
MYSTERY GIRLS HQ

Poppy's model poodle has gone. It was on her bag, by the kitchen door, a minute ago. But now we've looked in HQ too and we can't see it anywhere.

"It can't have just got up and walked off," Poppy said.

Violet looked scared when Poppy said that. "It's the curse – the poodle made the model poodle disappear to scare us," she said. "Listen! I can hear something upstairs."

Ruuff ruf.

"It's here! THE POODLE'S HERE! It's coming to get us!" Violet gasped.

"I can hear it too!" said Poppy. "Quick, get the camera!"

Hmmm. I could hear the bark too, but I wasn't sure this was a curse-related situation. Arthur had been suspiciously quiet for ages.

I checked the living room, where he was meant to be eating his tea. No Arthur. I raced upstairs.

Nothing could have prepared me for what I saw when I opened his bedroom door.

strange noise

Arthur was sitting on the floor having a picnic with his stuffed toys. And there, next to Mr Fluffy Face and Jeremiah Sock Monkey (used to be mine, before I became a serious detective), was Poppy's fake poodle!

"Ruuuf ruff … why, yes, Miss Misty-kins, of course I'll give you a second helping," Arthur said, pretending to pour tea and then trying to feed fish fingers to the poodle.

mr Fluffy face

Jeremiah sock monkey

UNBELIEVABLE!
Doesn't he know we're in the middle of an investigation?

"ARTHUR! WHAT are you doing with Mystery Girl property?" I said.

He looked up. And pulled the face he always pulls when he knows he's in trouble.

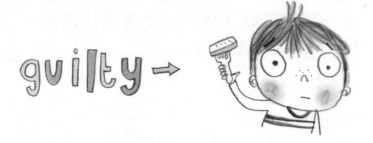

guilty →

"I, I … Mum says I need to try and stop being scared of the poodle before the sleepover on Saturday. Otherwise I can't go," he said.

"That doesn't explain why you are feeding fish fingers to a fake poodle!" I said.

"You've got ketchup on it!" said Poppy, horrified.

"I thought if I imagined the real poodle like this then it wouldn't seem so scary. And the poodle is meant to like being pampered!" said Arthur.

For a moment I didn't know what to say. Then it happened ...

A TOTALLY AMAZING IDEA ALERT!

The Young Super Sleuth's Handbook says it's important to keep your detective brain switched on at all times, especially when you have a difficult problem. Sometimes the answer can be right in front of your eyes.

"Arthur, you're brilliant!" I said. (I never say that.) "That's what we need to do to stop the curse!"

"What? Feed the poodle fish fingers?" said Violet.

"No!" I said. "Pay Misty compliments and be nice to her!"

"Amazing!" said Poppy. "That could be how we finish our presentation. 'And all it took was a bit of pampering to break the curse!'"

Who cares about the presentation? I'm, like, some sort of total detective genius!

Total genius

Friday 20th March

POOdle in the bath

Let Poodle Pampering commence!

Where is Rocky? Maybe if we break the curse he'll come back?

still LOST

12:30PM
PUDDLEFORD PRIMARY SCHOOL,
DINNER HALL

This is a strange sort of mystery. We have strong suspicions that the curse is active, but we haven't got any concrete evidence. If our plan to pamper the poodle works, we will have solved the case because there will be no more bad luck. But since no one seems to believe that the curse (or the case) exists, they are going to think we are crazy when we say we've solved it.

The Young Super Sleuth's Handbook says that a good detective stops people putting themselves in danger, even when they don't know they were in a dangerous situation in the first place.

We can't risk waiting until the sleepover tomorrow to pamper the poodle. We're going to the museum straight after school. I've packed the Mystery Kit:

Poodle Pampering kit:

PERFUME. (Lady Winkleton was posh so her poodle might have worn perfume.)

BOUNCY BALL.

BRUSH. (Also Watson's.)

WATSON'S CAT TREATS. (Mrs Finn's dog treats were all stolen.)

CUPCAKE. (Mum said we didn't have any caviar in this week when I asked.)

KNITTED CUSHION. (Looks comfy.)

DO NOT insult this POODLE!

DANGER: DO NOT INSULT THIS POODLE signs

I've got a good feeling about
this plan, but Violet isn't so sure.

Pom poms

"I'm not going unless we wear
these," Violet said, grabbing
a pair of bright pink socks with
pom-poms on from her bag.
"Lucky socks. Last time I wore
these, I managed to find the
pocket money I lost two weeks
ago. Down the back of the sofa.
I've got a pair for all of us."

pocket money

I'm not sure a pair of socks can be lucky but
me and Poppy have decided to wear them to
keep Violet happy.

I don't think this is what serious detectives
should be wearing, but we do need all the luck
we can get.

my rabbit socks

Poppys frog socks

"good doggie"

**4:30PM
PUDDLEFORD MUSEUM,
NATURAL PUDDLEFORD GALLERY**

This mission has been one of the Mystery Girls'
most dangerous yet. Here is my case report in full:

OPERATION HUG-A-POODLE

LOCATION: Winkleton's Wonders Gallery.

TEAM: Mystery Girls (and Daisy
Meadowfield, our woman on the inside).

Daisy

OBJECTIVE: To stop the poodle cursing
anyone else by pampering Misty and
making her feel loved, and to hang warning
signs to prevent any more incidences of poodle-
insulting.

3:40PM: Arriving at the museum, our first task is to persuade Daisy to help us. She says, "No way". But Poppy tells her it's her responsibility — something much worse than being locked in a toilet might happen to the poodle's next victim. Daisy agrees, but says she won't go anywhere near Misty.

3:42PM: Daisy takes one of Poppy's Young Super Sleuth walkie-talkies to the alarm control room and waits for our signal.

3:45PM: Violet's job is to distract museum security guard, Stanley. She begins by taking all the costumes off their hangers and trying them on. Stanley heads for the Dressing-Up Zone. Distraction successful.

Violet

3:50PM: I scatter dog treats on the floor around the poodle. Poppy says, "Wow, what a gorgeous creature! So cuuuute!" (I am astounded by her acting abilities — the poodle really is horrible.)

3:55PM: Violet has moved to the activity table now and is dropping crayons everywhere.

3:57PM: I give the signal to Daisy via the Young Super Sleuth walkie-talkie. "Who's a pretty doggy?" The buzzing of the alarm sensors disappears.

walkie-talkie

4:00PM: Ignoring Misty's creepy eyes, I tickle her chin and Poppy strokes her, just like we practised on the fake poodle last night.

tickle

stroke

4:01PM: Violet is refusing to pick up the crayons. Stanley is threatening to remove her from the museum.

4:02PM: Poppy sprays perfume and throws the cupcake on the floor. I place Fake Misty next to the real one so she can be close to her new friend. Then I say to Daisy, "Bedtime for puppies", and the alarm sensors begin to buzz again.

real misty

fake misty

4:03PM: Me and Poppy speed away to hide in the Natural Puddleford Gallery. Violet shouts, "That pupil just touched a stuffed tortoise!" Then she follows us out.

4:04PM: We see Stanley approach the poodle. He has just trodden on the cupcake and looks really angry. He doesn't spot Fake Misty though, or the warning sign. Ha!

4:10PM: Daisy walks past and winks. We don't consider new members often, but if she wants to, Daisy can totally join the Mystery Girls.

OUTCOME: MISSION SUCCESSFUL!

4:45PM
STILL IN NATURAL PUDDLEFORD GALLERY,
BEHIND SQUIRRELS INFORMATION BOARD

Phew! That was totally AMAZING detective work. We pampered the poodle and we did it without being cursed. (No sign of a bark.) Yessss!

Now all we have to do is watch. We've seen a few people looking at Misty, but we haven't heard any insults or, more importantly, barks.

Poppy says we'd better think about making props for the Museum Mayhem project. She thinks, since we've managed to stop the curse, we're in with a chance of winning.

Hang on! Visitor approaching the poodle.

5:30PM
MYSTERY GIRLS HQ

My Mystery Senses are telling me something isn't quite right. Not with the curse stuff, with something else.

I keep thinking about the last visitor we saw looking at the poodle. They were acting really weirdly.

I should have told Poppy and Violet about my suspicions at the museum but Mum was about to pick us up and Poppy wanted to make sure we had a plan for the sleepover tomorrow.

I've just made a sketch of what I observed.

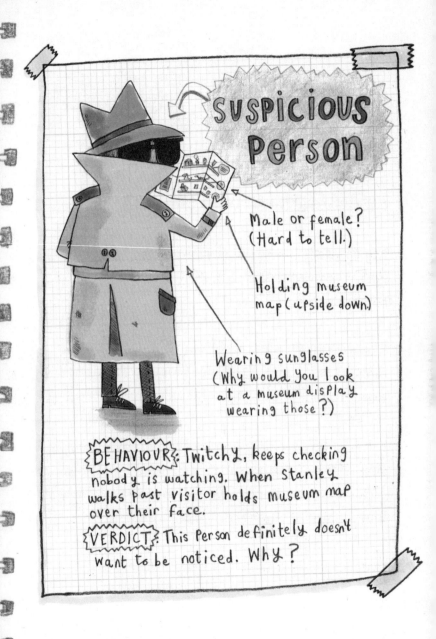

SUSPICIOUS Person

Male or female?
(Hard to tell.)

Holding museum
map (upside down.)

Wearing sunglasses
(Why would you look
at a museum display
wearing those?)

BEHAVIOUR: Twitchy, keeps checking
nobody is watching. When Stanley
walks past visitor holds museum map
over their face.

VERDICT: This person definitely doesn't
want to be noticed. Why?

6:10PM
MYSTERY GIRL HQ, BEAN BAG AREA

I've decided I can't get distracted with something that might not even be important – not when we've still got work to do.

I've written down our plan for the sleepover tomorrow. The Young Super Sleuth's Handbook says this is a good way to focus your Mystery Senses.

mystery senses

MUSEUM MAYHEM SLEEPOVER STRATEGY

OBJECTIVE: Ensure the poodle's curse has been contained and win Museum Mayhem competition.

PRIORITY 1: On arrival, make sure the 'DO NOT INSULT THIS POODLE' signs are still in place – without Stanley noticing.

PRIORITY 2: Keep the poodle under surveillance. There will be lots of people about and we can't risk any more mean comments being made. We don't know for sure yet whether we've stopped the curse for good.

PRIORITY 3: Deliver brilliant presentation, persuading everyone the curse did exist, and win the competition. Oh, and become world famous when our work is featured in the *Northern Star!*

Fame!

THE NORTHERN ★ STAR ★
MYSTERY GIRLS DO IT AGAIN!

my making a breakthrough face

8:10PM
22 SYCAMORE AVENUE, MY BEDROOM

I told Mum I needed to arrange an emergency
sleepover with Poppy and Violet but she said 'no
way' because we'd talk all night and be too tired
at the museum tomorrow. She's so annoying. I'm
investigating the weirdest, creepiest case we've
ever had. I DO NOT have time to be tired.

Since I left the museum, I've had questions
running through my head. Like, what if I wasn't
being paranoid? What if that person we saw at
the museum today was totally suspicious?

Then, while I was making an evidence board
for the presentation, Watson came in followed
by Arthur.

In his mouth, Watson had one of those stupid cardboard diamond necklaces Arthur keeps making.

"My diamond, my precious diamond!" Arthur cried, yanking the necklace out of Watson's mouth.

Cardboard diamond

Normally Arthur would be in SERIOUS trouble for barging into my bedroom, but I had a TOTALLY AMAZING REALISATION. The diamond. Why hadn't I thought of this before?

"Arthur! It's been right in front of us all along – THE DOG'S EYE DIAMOND!" I said.

Dog's Eye Diamond!

Arthur looked at me as if I'd gone crazy, but I didn't care. Why on earth would you be acting so secretively around an extremely expensive diamond? Unless . . . you were scoping the joint out* and totally plotting to come back and steal it!

If I'm even a bit right about any of this, somebody might be trying to steal the diamond NOW! By this time tomorrow, we could be too late. A curse and a potential diamond thief. It's a good job the curse has been broken – we could be totally busy investigating a diamond theft tomorrow!

*SCOPING THE JOINT OUT: This is when criminals check out a place (the joint) and plot how they could break in and steal something.

Saturday 21st March

ARRRGGggggHHHH!

Pickled Poisonous toads

**5:00PM
WINKLETON'S WONDERS GALLERY, BEHIND
DISPLAY OF PICKLED POISONOUS TOADS
(LYING LOW)**

I hardly got any sleep last night, worrying that
the suspicious person might have stolen the
diamond. It's OK, though – it's still here.

"Wouldn't the collar have been stolen by now
if there was a plot?" said Violet, when I told her
and Poppy my theory.

"Mariella, what evidence do we have of a plot to
steal the diamond other than one slightly
weird museum visitor yesterday?"
Poppy said.

sceptical

Hmmmm. I suppose we don't have any. I just have a funny feeling that something doesn't add up.

Unless the suspicious person is spotted again, we've decided to stick to the plan – keep the poodle under surveillance to stop any further poodle insults (and focus on our presentation).

A few people have walked right up to the poodle and pulled a bit of a face when they've seen it properly. (It's hard not to.) But our pampering and 'DO NOT INSULT THIS POODLE' sign seem to be working so far.

DO NOT INSULT THIS → POODLE

People have started to arrive for the sleepover now. Miss Twist, our really boring and sensible head teacher, is walking around wearing yellow floral pyjamas. Brilliant! And we almost didn't recognise Miss Crumble when we saw her – she is wearing bright pink polka-dot pyjamas!

Miss Crumble

We'd better get changed too. I thought if I was going to do a presentation persuading people a curse really exists while wearing pyjamas, I should wear my most serious pair. They are official Young Super Sleuth ones. (Not sure that Violet's kitten-print ones give the right impression.)

young Super Sleuth PJs

6:15PM
MUSEUM MAYHEM SLEEPOVER, MUSEUM ENTRANCE HALL (MAKE YOUR OWN LADY WINKLETON STYLE WIG ACTIVITY TABLE)

There are loads of totally cool activities happening before the presentations – like pickling your own poisonous toad (one made from clay, not a real one). And Sasha is here with the Perfect Pooches Dog Agility group. They are running a How to Dance With Dogs activity.

Sasha is wearing a pair of bright red silky pyjamas with a poodle's head sewn on the front. (I don't want to be mean but she does look a bit strange.)

poodle's head

I totally wanted to do the dog dancing activity, but we still need to monitor the poodle. From the Make Your Own Lady Winkleton Wig activity table we can see the stairs and the entrance to the Winkleton's Wonders Gallery.

string

WHAT is Arthur doing now? He keeps waving at us. He's on the Make Your Own Furry Poodle collage table. And – UNBELIEVABLE! He's wearing the same Young Super Sleuth pyjamas as me! Where did he get those? I'm going to have to have a word with Mum – Arthur is totally NOT a Young Super Sleuth!

What?

shock

STILL ON THE MAKE YOUR OWN LADY WINKLETON WIG ACTIVITY TABLE (IN SHOCK)

Arthur came over and started to show me the picture of a poodle he'd made.

"Look! It's Misty being pampered," he said.

At first I thought it was just a stupid wobbly scribble with googly eyes stuck on. Then I spotted something else.

Stuck to Arthur's picture with a huge blob of glue was a dog's collar and name tag. It said 'ROCKY'. What?

123

"WHERE DID YOU FIND THIS?" I said. We've been trying to figure out what's happened to Rocky all week. I couldn't believe Arthur had found a totally important bit of evidence right here in the museum!

"It looks really good, doesn't it?" Arthur said. "There's this bag at the end of the resources table with loads of cool stuff in – I found it in there."

He pointed to the bag. I recognised it straightaway – it was Sasha's bum bag! Why would Sasha have Rocky's collar in her bag? And why wouldn't she have told us about finding evidence like that?

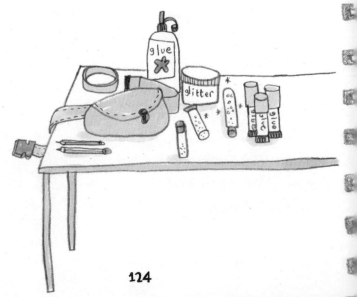

snooze
zone

6:42PM
MUSEUM ENTRANCE HALL. SNOOZE ZONE

The Young Super Sleuth's Handbook says that people only hide bits of evidence if they've got something to hide themselves.

"You don't think something has happened to Rocky and Sasha doesn't want to upset us by telling us, do you?" said Violet.

I looked at Sasha, just a few metres away, smiling and leading Bert through a dance to a really cheerful song. Surely she wouldn't be doing that if something awful had happened to Rocky?

"Maybe it's just in there from when Sasha was training Rocky?" said Poppy.

Of course, I thought. That's what it must be. But then I remembered. "It can't be! Jennifer told us Rocky was definitely wearing this collar when he went missing."

I spotted Jennifer's mum, Joyce, sitting by the dance floor, watching the Perfect Pooches. She looked totally miserable. Sasha and Joyce are meant to be friends, so why hadn't Sasha told her (or us) about the collar? I didn't want to say it, because I didn't want to believe it, but I had to.

JOYCE
(upset)

"Or Sasha knows where Rocky is. And she isn't telling us," I said.

shocked   stunned

6:50PM
MUSEUM ENTRANCE HALL, SCOPING OUT
RESOURCES TABLE

HUGE BREAKTHROUGH ALERT!

The dog dancing wasn't going to last forever and
we needed to check out Sasha's bum bag before
she put it back on again.

Suspecting Sasha felt like we were betraying
a friend, but we couldn't ignore the collar. The
Young Super Sleuth's Handbook says that people
close to an investigation *can* turn out to be the
culprits.

I walked towards the resources table. When I was
sure Sasha wasn't looking, I stuck my hand inside
the bag. This is what I pulled out.

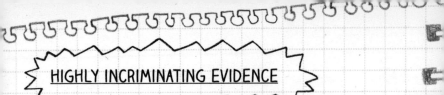

HIGHLY INCRIMINATING EVIDENCE

EXHIBIT A: Dark sunglasses
(Same ones worn by suspicious
person we saw yesterday.)

EXHIBIT B:
Deeply
incriminating
sketch

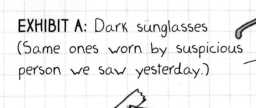

Alarm

MINE!
MINE!
MINE!
Alarm Sensors

TO DO - TARGETS

1. Daisy (airhead). ✓
2. Rocky. ✓
3. Short sighted Pet ✓
   Shop owner.
4. Stanley (annoying).
   TRY AGAIN?
5. MEDALLING MYSTERY
   GIRLS! (Still to do.)

EXHIBIT C: Totally
incriminating list.

I ♥ 💎

Fibber alert!

SASHA WINKLETON IS A TOTALLY MASSIVE, HUGE, FAKE FIBBER!

"It's her! She was the suspicious person yesterday and she wants the diamond. Those names on the list – they are all curse victims. I bet she's behind all the curse stuff too!" I said.

"What do you mean? I don't understand!" Violet said.

"Woah. Why are we are on that list?" said Poppy.

"All I know is if you wanted to steal a precious diamond, getting everyone worried about a curse would be the perfect way to distract people," I said. "And I don't know what she's got planned for us, but she won't get the chance to do it!"

The Perfect Pooches music stopped and everyone clapped. Apart from us. Sasha looked into the crowd and did a little bow. How could she stand there smiling? And what about Rocky? What has she done with him? Where is he?

Sasha spotted us and waved.

"Act natural," I whispered. "Pretend we totally like Sasha and don't know a thing."

I smiled and waved back. Poppy started grinning madly. Violet looked as if she'd just been cursed by the Pampered Poodle.

Sasha went to grab a treat for Bert, and it was then she realised she wasn't wearing her bum bag. For a moment, panic flashed across her face. I was pretending to be making a wig but I totally saw it. Guilty. Definitely guilty.

She spotted her bum bag on the resources table and dashed towards it. She looked inside, then clipped it back on and trotted over to chat with Beryl. Well, she isn't fooling us any more. Sasha Winkleton is totally under Mystery Girl surveillance.

GUILTY ALERT

THE MASTER CRIMINAL: HAVE YOU BEEN DUPED?

There is an old saying, keep your friends close, but your enemies closer. This is a saying familiar to many criminals. Suspects can be right under your nose, posing as innocent members of the public – a cunning trick to throw those investigating off their scent.

Signs of a Criminal Duper

1. A person involved with the investigation being very emotional or overly concerned. Are they trying to cover up their guilty conscience?

You can't suspect me! I look totally unsuspicious!

2. Somebody who finds lots of clues before you do – are they red herrings, designed to throw you off the scent of what is really happening?

LOOK! Evidence!

I have baked you some cakes.

3. Being helpful and offering assistance throughout the investigation. Does this person really want to help, or do they have an ulterior motive. Think before you let anyone into your circle of trust.

4. Nervous twitching and too much smiling. If it looks unnatural, it probably is.

Who stole that statue?

5. A person who repeatedly uses phrases like:

Whoever did this should be locked up!

If I just knew who did this I'd make sure they got into a whole world of trouble.

WARNING

Remember, these could all be the signs of a very helpful member of the public. Make sure you have evidence before making accusations.

Prepare for utter unbelievable-ness! I didn't get time to write in my journal after I made the discovery in Sasha's bag. This is an accurate account of what happened next.

The Museum Entrance Hall

Operation Sneaky Sleepover

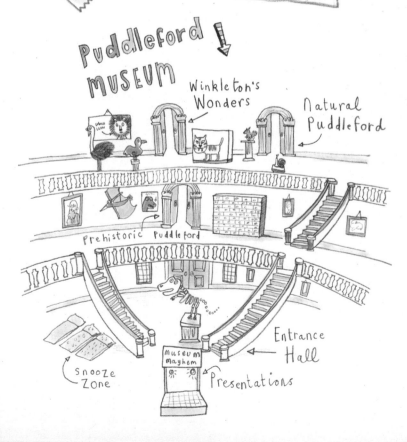

Puddleford MUSEUM

Winkleton's Wonders

Natural Puddleford

Prehistoric Puddleford

Entrance Hall

Snooze Zone

museum mayhem

Presentations

7:05PM
MUSEUM ENTRANCE HALL

Before we could decide what to do, Miss Twist was telling everyone to gather in their sleeping bags for the presentations. I could see Sasha laughing and chatting with Miss Crumble at the back of the hall, as if they were best friends.

"It can't be true! Sasha wouldn't do this!" said Violet.

I couldn't blame Violet for still being in denial about Sasha. She'd been so nice it was hard to accept. But being nice was just part of her cover and I knew now that she'd been lying to us all along.

"Think about it, Violet. She's been hanging around the museum loads. She could have locked Daisy in the toilet and got Bert to bark – it must have been his paw print we found," I said.

"That fur in Fluff 'n' Feathers could have been Bert's too. He's a black poodle. How did we not think of that?" Poppy said, shaking her head.

"But – Rocky! Does she still have him?" said Violet. "And why does she want the diamond? Was it her who pushed over Ginger Gertie? What is she planning to do to us?"

I was about to say that, actually, I don't have all the answers, all of the time, when Poppy nudged me.

"Erm, can anyone actually see Sasha?" she said.

EMPty!

7:15PM
IN THE MUSEUM LIFT, HEADED FOR
WINKLETON'S WONDERS GALLERY

We had to find Sasha. The trouble was, we were stuck in our sleeping bags in front of the whole school.

"I don't like this!" said Violet. "We should tell a teacher!"

I saw a flash of pink pyjamas next to me. Miss Crumble.

"Ssshhhhhh, girls. You're disturbing the presentations," she said. "And what do you want to tell a teacher?"

I wouldn't normally fib, but this was an emergency. Sasha could have run off with the diamond by now, for all we knew.

"Violet doesn't feel well, Miss. I think it's nerves, you know, with the pressure of the competition. Can we take her to the toilets?"

Pale

Miss Crumble sighed. "OK, girls, but be quick. Your slot is coming up soon."

Before she could change her mind, Poppy grabbed Violet by the elbows, and I picked up the Mystery Kit. We ran towards the lift that would take us to the Winkleton's Wonders Gallery.

That's where we were sure Sasha would be headed too.

Everything in the museum looked totally spooky now that it was dark. There were weird shadows that would make the perfect hiding place for Sasha Winkleton, ruthless diamond thief and dognapper.

The Pampered Poodle looked extra creepy as the lasers of the alarm system cast a flickering green glow over it. You couldn't see them during the day, but now there were zigzagging green lights whizzing around.

I watched a spy film once, called *The Mystic Moustache* (starring ace detective Carrie Clew), where priceless objects were protected by laser light beams. I knew if anyone tried to cross them, the alarms would go off.

"Are we sure that thing isn't cursed? I mean — it looks as if it is," said Violet.

"Looks can be deceptive," I said.

RrrrRUF!

Violet, Poppy and I stared at each other, and then at the poodle. Its eyes flickered in the whizzing laser beams.

It had sounded as if the bark had come from the poodle. It was short, snappy and angry, just as our witnesses had described.

"The curse!" Violet whispered, gripping my arm.

RrrrRUF!

Poppy gasped and jumped back. The bark was louder this time, and this time it definitely hadn't come from the poodle. No, it seemed to be coming from behind us. Along the corridor.

"It's not the poodle! It must be Sasha and Bert! They're coming for the diamond!" I said. My voice echoed spookily around the dark gallery. "Follow that bark!"

We slipped out of the Winkleton's Wonders Gallery and onto the balcony overlooking the entrance hall. Alice and Jane from Year Six were singing their song about Lady Winkleton's tortoises. It was awful, but at least nobody would notice we were missing with all that screeching going on.

RrrrRUF!

The bark was fainter now. I could only just hear it over the singing. Was it coming from the floor below? We tiptoed down the staircase, staying in the shadows in case anyone at the sleepover spotted us.

RrrrRUF!

There it was again.
Louder this time.
And coming from
Prehistoric Puddleford.
We sprinted past
the dinosaur
skeletons and fossils
and then . . .

Prehistoric man

caveman

7:35PM
PREHISTORIC PUDDLEFORD GALLERY

Silence. The only sound now was a faint clapping from downstairs.

"If that bark was Bert and Sasha, where are they?" whispered Poppy. "Maybe we were wrong. Maybe we should just get back to the presentation."

What? We couldn't give up now. Not after everything Sasha had done! That bark definitely sounded as if it had come from in here.

"I don't get it. Why would Sasha be in here if she wants the diamond upstairs?" said Violet.

Violet was right. It seemed weird that we'd followed Sasha down here, when she was plotting to steal the diamond upstairs. Unless . . .

"IT'S A TRICK!" I said. "It must be! She wants us out of the way so she can get to the diamond!"

My 'utterly annoyed at being tricked' face

7:38PM
WINKLETON'S WONDERS GALLERY

We sprinted back up the stairs to the Winkleton's Wonders Gallery and skidded through the doorway. The exhibition was as dark and quiet as before. It was as if the weird creatures on display were lurking, waiting to pounce from the shadows. Was Sasha here too?

I looked at the poodle. The diamond twinkled. Lasers danced around its greenish fur. Its eyes glowed in the darkness. I looked closer. Slowly, spookily, the Pampered Poodle turned its head.

ARGgggggHHHhhhhHHH!

THINKING LIKE A DETECTIVE: COPING IN SCARY SITUATIONS

You've read your Young Super Sleuth's Handbook and rehearsed a million times what you would do when faced with a scary situation. But when the moment comes, will you be able to stay and face danger? Or will you run screaming from the room and miss vital clues?

Train Your Brian to Handle Fear Like a Detective

Fearless

1. Imagine the thing that is scaring you is actually a fluffy pink kitten.

Scary

Non-scary

2. Call for back up or reassurance on a Young Super Sleuth walkie-talkie.

MYSTERY SITUATION CONFIRMED!

3. Whistle a happy tune to distract yourself from what is happening.

Discovering Famous Detectives: Franny the Fearless

Franny Framer laughed in the face of fear. She was the only private investigator fearless enough to prove that reports a hair salon was haunted by a gruesome severed hairdresser's head were false. Franny was able to confront the severed head without being even slightly scared. She proved it was in fact just a hairdresser's dummy head covered in ketchup. The whole terrifying episode had been an elaborate trick played by a jealous rival hairdressing salon.

TOP TIP

If you find a spider in the bath, practise getting close to it without screaming. Can you pick it up? If so, you are well on your way to being **FEARLESS**!

7:42PM
WINKLETON'S WONDERS GALLERY (AGAIN)

"Ruuuunn!" screamed Violet, sprinting towards the exit.

Poppy pulled my arm. "COME ON!" she shouted.

Even though seeing the Pampered Poodle come to life was totally the most scary thing ever, before I ran away I grabbed the camera from the Mystery Kit and pointed it at the poodle.

The flash went off, lighting up the whole room. The Dog's Eye Diamond glinted. That was weird. Why was the poodle holding its collar in its mouth? Then I realised.

150

"ROCKY! That isn't the poodle – it's Rocky!"
I yelled.

Poppy and Violet stopped in the doorway
and turned.

It was hard to see in the eerie
green light, but there, sitting
on the Pampered Poodle's
stand next to Misty, was
Rocky, the diamond collar
sparkling in his mouth.

ROCKY!

How had he got up there?
Why was he up there?
And why weren't the
alarms going off?

Before any of us could speak,
Rocky leaped forwards.
He landed on the floor,
centimetres from a beam of
green light. I held my breath
and waited for the alarm to
sound.

Rocky looked around, as if he wasn't sure where to go. Suddenly, he did a triple backflip, landing on his back paws out of reach of the laser. Then he darted past my feet, like a hairy shadow, and sped towards the door. He was getting away! With the diamond!

"Stop!" Poppy shouted.

"No!" I called.

"Rocky?" Violet said in disbelief.

Rocky glanced back at Violet. He'd recognised his name!

"Rockeeey!! Good boy, come here, Rockeey!" I said, pulling the bag of cat treats from the Mystery Kit.

For a moment I thought he would ignore me, then Rocky stopped and turned, wagging his tail.

"Come on, boy, treeeeats!" I called again. He dropped the collar and trotted towards me.

"The collar! GET IT!" I yelled to Poppy and Violet. (They were frozen to the spot, like a pair of stuffed exhibits.)

Violet grabbed the diamond and held it in the air. "I've got it! I've got it!" she said.

"Woah. This is the weirdest case we've EVER investigated!" said Poppy, looking first at Rocky eating the treats out of my hand, then at Violet.

Suddenly, we heard a voice I'd sort of been expecting to hear ever since we'd arrived in the Winkleton's Wonders Gallery.

"Good evening, Mystery Madams. Enjoying your little pyjama party with my star pupil?" said Sasha.

7:50PM
WINKLETON'S WONDERS GALLERY (WITH A CRAZED RELATIVE OF LADY WINKLETON)

Sasha was standing in the doorway, smiling weirdly. The green glow of the lasers reflected off her red silky pyjamas. Bert was in her arms. He bared his teeth and growled.

"You may as well give up now, because you aren't getting that diamond!" I said, trying to sound totally confident. (I was actually pretty scared. Who knew what Sasha would do now that we were onto her?)

Sasha sniggered. "What do you think, Bert?" she said. "Shall we just leave that diamond and go back to being dog trainers?"

Bert jumped out of her arms.
Taking a step towards us,
he growled again.

"No, I didn't think so,
Bert," Sasha continued.
"That collar is MINE! My
great-great-grandmother
was an idiot! What was
she thinking, giving away our
family's fortune to this STUPID
dusty old museum of JUNK?"

Her hair was sticking up all over the place, and
her eyes were glowing in the green light.

"The Dog's Eye Diamond belongs to ME – and I
intend to take it!" She pointed at Violet, who was
still clutching the collar.

Rocky was sitting at Poppy's feet, licking his bum,
as if there wasn't anything even a bit unusual
about this situation.

"It's too late, Sasha," I said, putting on my best 'you've messed with the wrong detective' voice. "The Dog's Eye Diamond is under Mystery Girl protection now."

"Don't even begin to think you've got this all figured out! What sort of detectives would follow Bert's bark downstairs if they believed I was after the diamond?" Sasha spat. "Ha! The same stupid detectives who believed this mangy old poodle was cursed, that's who! Well, you stupid meddling Mystery Girls, it was ME, all along!"

Poppy gasped. (Sasha was confirming what we already knew, but it was still shocking to hear it.)

scary

"You seem to be forgetting, we're here now and we're going to stop you!" I said.

"As if you could! I bet you still haven't figured out that I snatched Rocky to get past that stupid alarm system. Bert's good, but not quite as good at triple backflips as Rocky," Sasha said. "Now give me that diamond!"

"NO WAY!" said Violet, holding the diamond to her. "We'll tell everyone it was you all along."

Violet

"Ah, but you see, nobody will believe you," Sasha said. "The little Project File I've left downstairs for your teachers will see to that."

Poppy stepped forward. "I don't know what you're talking about, but if you've ruined our chances in the competition, I'll, I'll . . ."

"You'll what? Tell Beryl that you weren't plotting to steal the diamond tonight? I'm afraid the Project File says something VERY different," Sasha said. "And by the time anyone realises you're innocent, I'll be long gone!"

Sasha reached in her bum bag and pulled out something small and shiny. Her whistle.

She blew into it. Rocky and Bert were suddenly alert. They both turned and growled at us. Then they yapped and jumped forwards, forcing us further into the gallery.

"I think you'd better hand me that collar, don't you?" said Sasha.

As we edged away from the growling dogs, the packet of cat treats in my pocket rustled. Of course! It was my last chance and I had to take it.

"Treats! Treeeeeats!" I called, throwing the whole bag on the floor. They scattered everywhere, but Bert and Rocky didn't take their eyes off us. It hadn't worked! Was this the end for the Mystery Girls?

7:50PM
WINKLETON'S WONDERS GALLERY
TRYING TO ESCAPE CRAZED DIAMOND THIEF

Rocky's nose twitched. He smelled the treats!
He snapped out of his scary trance and started
hoovering them up. Bert's eyes flickered from us
to the treats, then he dived on them too.

Sasha blew furiously on her whistle.

"RUN!" I yelled to Poppy and Violet. We darted
past Sasha, towards the door.

"Give me that collar, NOW!" she screamed.

Ruuuff, ruff!

The treats were gone. Rocky and Bert were after us again, snapping at our heels.

Now I heard the thud of Sasha's slippers and the swish of her pyjamas getting closer. I glanced behind. Her arms were outstretched, her eyes fixed on the diamond in Violet's hands. Any moment now she'd be close enough to snatch it, and the dogs would be on to us.

We needed to distract them. But how? We were almost at the huge wooden doors to the gallery when I had a moment of detective genius.

"THROW IT!" I called to Violet. "Throw the collar into the lasers!"

Violet didn't need telling twice.
She launched threw the collar
over her shoulder.

Sasha staggered to a halt. Her eyes fixed on the diamond flying through the air.

Woohooowoohoowoohoooh!

The diamond had crossed the lasers. It sailed over Sasha's head and skidded across the floor.

Bert and Rocky tried to change direction and go after the collar, but on the shiny floor they just skidded through the gallery doors after us.

"DOORS! Get the doors!" I yelled over the alarm.

Poppy and Violet pushed one of the heavy wooden doors, I threw myself against the other.

Crrrrreeeeak! BANG!

The doors closed, I flicked the latch.
Sasha was trapped.

Sasha
TRAPPED
HA!

162

8:00PM
JUST OUTSIDE WINKLETON'S WONDERS
GALLERY. CRAZED DIAMOND THIEF
CONTAINED.

"ROCKY!" somebody screamed.

It was Jennifer. She was running up the stairs
in her pyjamas, along with most of our school.
Miss Crumble was with her and I could just
about hear Beryl's voice over the alarms and
the excited crowd. She was shouting,
"EVACUATE THE MUSEUM!" But
nobody was listening.

Jennifer

Rocky jumped into Jennifer's
arms and licked her face.
Joyce looked as if she might
cry when she saw them.

Bert was lying
down outside the
gallery, yawning
as though nothing
had happened.

"WHAT on earth do you
girls think you are doing?"
screamed Beryl, as she pushed her way to the
front, followed closely by Stanley and Daisy.

"Ah, Beryl," I said. (There was no way I was
letting her tell me off after we'd just saved her
museum from losing the Dog's Eye Diamond.)
"I must inform you there has been a plot to
steal the Dog's Eye Diamond."

"What rubbish," snapped Stanley.

"If you don't believe me, you'll find the thief,
Sasha Winkleton, trapped in there," I said,
pointing at the doors.

"WHAT? First you set off the alarms, and now you've made up some insane story about poor Sasha Winkleton," said Beryl.

cross

Just then, the alarm cut out and there was silence. Beyond the doors, we heard a shout.

"MINE! THE DIAMOND IS MINE! HA HA haaa!"

Beryl looked confused. "Is that . . .?"

"Yes, Beryl. That is Sasha Winkleton," I said. "She's been stringing you all along, pretending there is a curse, so she can steal the Dog's Eye Diamond."

Everyone gasped. I love it when I get to shock everyone with our mystery-solving skills!

"Just another job for the Mystery Girls – able to solve any mystery, even wearing our pyjamas!" I said, grinning at Poppy and Violet.

my → smug face

Sunday
22nd March

We did it! We solved the case.
(Not quite the one we expected
to, but we still **TOTALLY
SOLVED** it!)

saved?

2:30PM
MYSTERY GIRLS HQ

When everyone from school found out we'd stopped a diamond theft as part of our Museum Mayhem project, they were totally impressed and wanted to hear our presentation.

While we were waiting for the Puddleford police to turn up and arrest Sasha we totally spooked some of the younger kids telling them about the bit when we thought there really was a curse.

Spooked!

The judge from the *Northern Star* said that our investigation was really creepy, but was more about how Sasha had made the whole curse thing up than the actual poodle. Poppy was fuming when Jane and Alice in Year Six won the prize. Then – TOTALLY AMAZING – the judge offered to feature our Dog's Eye Diamond investigation as a lead story.

The police said the museum was a crime scene and they needed witness statements from everyone. Nobody was allowed to leave until morning, which turned out to be great because we still got to sleep in the museum!

It was a once-in-a-lifetime thing because I overheard Beryl say that there was absolutely NO WAY she'd EVER allow another sleepover at the museum.

But the weirdest thing by far was what happened when the police arrived. Sasha had been quiet for ages and when Detective Sparks opened the doors to the gallery, the Dog's Eye Diamond was back around the poodle's neck and Sasha was nowhere to be seen.

At first they thought she'd escaped, then Beryl spotted her, stuck under the portrait of Misty and Lady Winkleton. When she was freed, Sasha begged Detective Sparks to take her away from 'that poodle'. C-r-e-e-p-y alert!

Fallen from wall

help!

Could it be that the poodle really *is* cursed? I don't think we'll ever be one hundred per cent sure. But after piecing together the clues and evidence we found, we now know EXACTLY how Sasha made it look like a curse to cover her plot to steal the Dog's Eye Diamond.

CASE REPORT:
THE CURSE OF THE PAMPERED POODLE

All reports of curse-related activity over the past week can be traced back to Sasha Winkleton, great-great-granddaughter of museum founder and Pampered Poodle owner, Lady Winkleton.

Sasha was angry that Lady Winkleton had donated her family's fortune to the museum, along with the priceless Dog's Eye Diamond. She'd grown up listening to her father saying if it wasn't for the stupidity of Lady Winkleton they would have been totally rich.

Sasha plotted to steal the diamond when it was returned to Puddleford for the museum's anniversary. When Sasha noticed how many people were interested in the spooky curse stories, she realised this was the perfect cover for her terrible plans.

Sasha's first attempt to steal the diamond failed, setting the museum's alarms off. (And cancelling our school trip.) Her attempt to disable the alarm by spilling coffee on it didn't work either.

Coffee →

Bert →

We know of three witnesses Sasha fooled into thinking they were cursed – Daisy, Jennifer's mum, Joyce, and Mrs Finn. They all thought they had heard the poodle's bark, when they actually heard Bert's. Sasha also attempted to scare Stanley away from the diamond by pushing over a seven-foot-tall ginger polar bear right next to him.

Sasha realised her best chance to get past the alarm was to use her most talented and agile pupil, Rocky, so she dognapped him. (Using her whistle to make him run off.)

She practised controlling Rocky by breaking into Fluff 'n' Feathers and getting him to steal the expensive posh collar from the display. Bert was there too — that's why we found his paw print and fur.

ROCKY

Sasha decided to put her plan into action on Saturday night, when she knew the museum staff would be distracted by the Museum Mayhem sleepover.

She came to the museum in a disguise the day before to do a last check of the alarm system. But she didn't count on the Mystery Girls being there too. Spotting the suspicious figure, we quickly realised there could be something funny going on.

totally suspicious →

bumbag

Sasha's final mistake was leaving her bum bag, filled with incriminating evidence, unattended. That's what led us to rumbling her terrible plot to steal the diamond.

Weird

We still can't be sure if curses are real or not. What happened to Sasha after she had been contained in the Winkleton's Wonders Gallery makes us think that there is definitely something not right about that poodle. And if curses are real, it's very hard to prove, even if you are a Mystery Girl. But we would like to let everyone know that Puddleford is a Pampered Poodle curse-free zone and normal levels of luck should now resume.

CASE CLOSED.

Mystery Girls
with the diamond!

If you are still
worried about bad
luck we recommend
wearing lucky socks.

Lucky
socks

the
orion star

Sign up for
newsletter to get inside information
about your favourite children's authors
as well as exclusive competitions and
early reading copy giveaways.

www.orionbooks.co.uk/newsletters

Follow on

Orion
Children's Books